The Snow Queen

CARLTON
BOOKS

Long ago in a little town, freezing winter came. All along the chimney pots, over the cobbles and white rooftops, snow fell soft on snow. Nothing stirred, except for the wind that whipped round corners and down alleyways.

In a grey doorway a ragged boy shivered. His name was Kay and he was all alone, his only friend a little flute that he played for company. The stuttering notes fell onto the air, to be snatched by the wind and carried off. And poor Kay was pinched by the devilish cold.

Out of the gloom two figures appeared, hurrying in the chill. It was Gerda and her mother coming home to light the fires.

"Mother," said the girl, "that boy looks so unhappy."

"Give him this," replied the woman, "but hurry up, Gerda, it's cold."

Gerda pressed a coin into Kay's shivering hand, and its warmth comforted him.

The night grew colder still and snow swirled all about. From her bedroom window, Gerda watched the thick snowflakes.

"They're like a million white bees," said her mother.

"Then there must be a queen somewhere?" asked Gerda.

Her mother answered in a hushed voice, "Yes, she is the Snow Queen. Her touch is colder than the devil's kiss. That's what your grandfather used to say. You can't see her, but she's out there watching, where the storm is busiest."

Gerda shivered at the thought. She couldn't forget about the poor boy outside. When her mother left the room, she crept to the window, opened it, and threw a soft white blanket down to him. Kay was grateful for this small kindness. He wrapped the blanket tightly around himself, and settled down to rest.

Snow fell fast on snow, and the boy sank into sleep. In the eerie silence only snowflakes drifted by. Then, out of the dark, flew a glistening sledge, pulled by five white swans, and on it sat a beautiful lady, glittering like ice. Her skin was pale, her eyes were black and restless as the wind. She wore a cloak of billowing snow, and she sparkled with bright jewels. It was the Snow Queen. She had come for Kay, and beckoned him to come away.

Suddenly a bright light shone and woke Kay from his dream. The snow still fell, but the Snow Queen had gone. Kay felt a gentle hand on his arm, warm and comforting.

"Come inside," said Gerda's mother. "You can stay with us tonight."

And so it was that Kay found a home, and lived with Gerda and her mother. Winter was no longer cold and dark, but a magical world of white. Every day Kay played with Gerda, sledging and making snowmen. No children were ever happier than these kind and loving friends.

Until one day, when everything changed.

Kay was in the forest pulling Gerda on her sledge. Along the track were Pieter and Stefan, the naughtiest boys in the town. They had tied their sledges to a farmer's cart, and were being pulled along in the snow. They mocked and laughed at the poor farmer, who was innocent of their tricks. Kay's heart beat with excitement.

"Look how fast they're going!" he thought. "I want to do that too." But before he could join in their cruel fun, the boys sped past and were gone.

That night Kay and Gerda sat by the window. The snow fell like a thick blanket.

"I wonder if the Snow Queen is watching us," said Gerda. "Mother says her heart is colder than ice."

"I've seen her," said Kay. "She's more beautiful than you can imagine, and sparkles like diamonds. When she comes here I will let her in, then you can see her too."

"You haven't seen her!" laughed Gerda, as her mother joined them at the window. "And anyway, if she does come, I shall melt her on the stove!"

Kay felt a stab of anger. Why didn't Gerda believe him? That night he tossed and turned in bed. "You wait, I'll show you," he thought angrily.

Suddenly an eerie light glowed outside in the darkness. Kay crept out of bed and opened the window. A blizzard raged and snowflakes pelted down, sharp like icy splinters. As Kay looked up one flew into his eye, and he felt a searing pain. "There's something in my eye!" he screamed, and blood trickled down his cheek. Outside, in the whirling flurry, the icy Snow Queen smiled.

Gerda, woken by the noise, ran to the window and shut it. "What's the matter, Kay?" she said to her friend, but Kay turned on her in a fury.

"Leave me alone, you stupid girl. Go away and let me sleep!" Gerda was hurt by his vicious words, and hot tears filled her eyes.

When morning came Kay's bed was empty and Gerda's sledge had gone. The sullen boy had slipped away and left the sleeping girl behind. Kay didn't want to play with Gerda any more or join in her silly games. He wanted to laugh and make fun of people, like his new friends Pieter and Stefan did.

Later that day, when Kay was playing with his new friends, a strange noise came from the sky, like the rushing of winter winds.

Suddenly behind the trees a crystal sledge flew past. A dazzling woman dressed in white looked towards the boys. It was the Snow Queen! Quick as a flash Kay grabbed his sledge and tied it onto hers. Pieter and Stefan watched in awe as their friend was whisked away. When Gerda came to look for him, she asked the boys where he was.

"He's gone," said Pieter. "He went towards the river."

High above in the leaden sky, the Snow Queen and Kay rode away to the north.

Far below Gerda called for Kay but there was no reply. All that was left of him was the little sledge which fell from the sky and crashed, unseen, into the silent river.

Soon the town was green again with the first buds of spring, and the warm sun shone, and the river flowed once more. Down on the jetty a fisherman caught a rusty sledge in his net. When Gerda and her mother saw it they were sure that Kay had drowned.

The lonely girl wept bitter tears for her dearest, lost companion. She cried to the sky, to the birds and the trees to tell her if it was true. She even cried to the river.

"If only you could speak," sighed Gerda.

"I can speak," said a raven, perched nearby. "Why are you crying?" he said.

Gerda told the raven about Kay and how he had died in the river.

"He is not dead," said the raven. "I know, because I see everything."

"Where did he go?" said Gerda. "How can I find him?"

"Go north," replied the raven. "Let the river take you." And he flew away.

So Gerda climbed into the little boat by the jetty, and set off along the river.

On and on the river carried her, away from the town and her mother. Hours passed, and the riverbanks turned to meadows and ancient trees. It seemed to Gerda like a magical picture that changed as she drifted by. On and on the river flowed, leaving everything behind it, and Gerda fell into a tranquil sleep, lulled by its gentle rhythm.

When she woke, the boat had stopped at the end of a beautiful garden. It was full of flowers of every kind. Under a tree a table was set, as if someone was having tea. An old woman came out of a cottage. She smiled as if she had been expecting Gerda.

"Now my dear, do sit down and tell me why you are here," she said.

Gerda told the old woman all about Kay and how she was looking for him.

"I haven't seen him, but I am sure he will be here soon. Let's have some cake," said the old woman. "I'll just go inside and get a knife to cut it."

In the garden there were tiny whispers. "Little girl! Over here." Gerda saw that a rose was calling to her. She bent and touched its petals.

"Oh, beautiful rose, have you seen my friend, Kay?"

All the flowers in the garden whispered at once. "We are the flowers that know the earth best. Your friend is not dead. He lies in rest, hidden in a palace, but he is not free. Hurry now, leave this enchanted place."

The old woman came out of the house, and saw Gerda talking to the rose. "Come here!" she shouted, grabbing Gerda's wrist.

"Ouch! You're hurting me!" said Gerda, as the talking raven suddenly appeared. With a raucous flapping, the raven flew at the old woman.

"Run, Gerda, run," the raven squawked, and they fled the enchanted garden.

Behind them the furious old woman gave one sweep of her cake knife, and chopped the head off the beautiful rose.

Gerda ran as fast as she could, fighting through thickets and thorns in the surrounding forest. Bedraggled and bleeding, Gerda stopped for breath. The raven flew to a tree.

The raven called down to Gerda, "I can see a palace!"

"Perhaps it is where Kay is hidden," said Gerda. "We must go there."

The tangled forest gave way to a palace guarded by ancient statues. There was a terrible grinding of rock as one came to life and spoke. "What is your business here?" it boomed. Gerda explained that she was looking for Kay.

"A boy did come here before last spring," said the statue. "Today he marries the princess. You may enter, but hurry, the feast is about to begin."

Gerda ran through the halls of the palace as fast as her legs could go. She burst into the wedding feast and pushed to the front of the crowd. The king was sitting on his throne, and before him stood a girl and a boy. "I've found Kay!" gasped Gerda. But when the boy turned to look at her, she saw that it was not Kay at all. Gerda fell to the floor and cried as if her heart would break.

Later that night, when she had recovered, Gerda told her story.

"It sounds to me as if your friend wanted to go with her," said the king.

"No!" cried Gerda. "Kay was bewitched by the Snow Queen, that's why he went."

"I think there is a darker magic at work here," said the king. And he told Gerda the story of a wicked magician and his evil mirror.

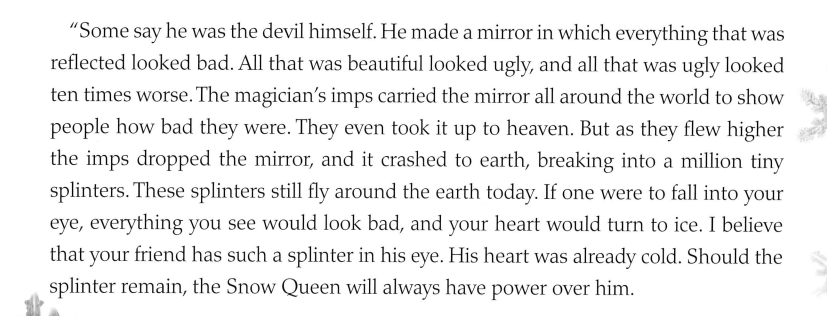

"Some say he was the devil himself. He made a mirror in which everything that was reflected looked bad. All that was beautiful looked ugly, and all that was ugly looked ten times worse. The magician's imps carried the mirror all around the world to show people how bad they were. They even took it up to heaven. But as they flew higher the imps dropped the mirror, and it crashed to earth, breaking into a million tiny splinters. These splinters still fly around the earth today. If one were to fall into your eye, everything you see would look bad, and your heart would turn to ice. I believe that your friend has such a splinter in his eye. His heart was already cold. Should the splinter remain, the Snow Queen will always have power over him.

Gerda looked sad, but the king comforted her. "Do not despair, child, you have a power far greater than hers," he said. "It comes from your heart. Your love is that of an innocent child, and no dark power is mightier than that."

Gerda did not understand what the king meant, but she was too tired to think and lay down to rest.

The next morning, the princess gave Gerda her best fur cape and boots. The king ordered a royal coach to take her on the journey. Gerda thanked them and set off into the forest. But the road was rough, and the carriage rocked as it rattled over stony ground. The sky grew dark, and storm clouds gathered.

As thunder rumbled, lightning flashed, and the wild wind whipped around. The carriage came to a halt. Up ahead on the forest track lay a woman's lifeless body. Gerda jumped down from the carriage.

Suddenly the coach was surrounded by fierce robbers, and the woman sprang up. As she held a knife at Gerda's throat, a rough voice screamed, "Leave her alone, she's mine!"

Gerda saw that it was a filthy child who looked wilder than a tiger. She was the woman's daughter. Gerda was taken back to their camp by the robbers, who drank and danced like demons. Gerda was very afraid.

"They won't kill you," said the robber girl, "as long as you do as I say. Are you a princess?"

Gerda said she was not a princess, and told the robber girl her story. The robber girl felt sorry for Gerda. She was just a lonely child who wanted a friend. So when Gerda promised to be her friend forever, she agreed to help her.

"Take that reindeer," said the ragged girl. "He is very clever and will take you north. But wait until everyone is asleep."

So when everyone finally went to sleep, Gerda climbed onto the reindeer, and held on tight as they galloped off into the night.

On and on they rode, through forests, and valleys, and hills. Days and nights came endlessly, and spring and summer passed. Autumn fell in a flourish of leaves. Vast plains gave way to mountains, and the ground grew frosty and bare. Far to the north freezing winter covered everything in white.

On and on they traveled until Gerda could go no further. Numbed with cold, she collapsed into the snow. Then out of the storm came a lumbering beast. It grabbed the frozen child by her cloak, and dragged her away.

When Gerda woke, she lay in a room where a huge fire crackled and blazed. All around were oil lamps and fish that hung from the rafters. In a shadowy corner a figure moved, then turned to look at the girl. It was the beast that had dragged her from the snow, and Gerda was sure it would eat her. But, instead, the figure reached up and pulled off a bearskin hood, to reveal the face of a smiling woman beneath. It was the Finland woman, and she had rescued Gerda from the cold.

"Here," she said, "have some food." Gerda ate ravenously, and, in between mouthfuls she told the woman how she came to be half dead in the snow.

"Do you know how to get to the Snow Queen?" asked Gerda.

The woman looked a little afraid. "Not exactly," she said.

Gerda began to cry. "Kay needs my help. I must find him," she sobbed.

The Finland woman soothed the girl. "There, there, my child," she crooned. "I don't have the power to get you to the Snow Queen. You need the help of the Laplander for that. I can show you where to find her."

The woman unrolled a map full of strange markings and lines. She ran her finger along the lines, pointing to the markings, and told Gerda to listen carefully.

"Go north across the great river. It is a treacherous place, so be very careful. Then you must pass through the tunnel of sound. If you survive that, there is a great mountain to climb. Beyond it is the land of the midnight sun, that is where you will find the Lapland woman."

Gerda and the reindeer pushed on through arctic winds and deep, relentless snow. After many miles they came to the great river, and crossed the huge ice flow.

Exhausted and freezing, Gerda and the reindeer arrived at the entrance to the tunnel of sound. Inside they were deafened by screeching echoes. They fought their way through blasting winds and blinding colors. At last, the travelers left the howling screams behind, and stepped outside into the eerie silence.

There in front of them stood a vast mountain, its peak disappearing up into the clouds. There was no time to stop, so Gerda and the reindeer started to climb the mountain's treacherous heights. At the top they could see for miles across a plain of perpetual winter. All was frozen and white in the land of the midnight sun.

"Look! Over there! I can see the Lapland woman's house," said Gerda, pointing at a solitary igloo that glowed with flickering lights. From inside came a low chanting sound that echoed, as if from a dream. Gerda entered the little snow house, and greeted the Lapland woman.

"The Finland woman sent me to you," said Gerda. "I am looking for my friend, Kay, who was taken by the Snow Queen. Can you help me find her palace?" she asked. A long time seemed to pass as she waited for a reply.

The Lapland woman looked at Gerda, then spoke in a low, hushed voice. "The place you seek is beyond the northern lights," she said. "It is a very long way to travel. Drink this special potion, and it will speed you on your way." And the Lapland woman offered Gerda a cup of liquid that sparkled like a million tiny stars.

"This potion is very powerful," explained the Lapland woman. "It will take you to the Snow Queen herself. But be warned, her power is stronger than all the winds of the world tied together."

Gerda's heart beat wildly, and she felt afraid. "I can't give up now," she thought. "Kay is my dearest friend and he needs my help. I must find the Snow Queen."

With shaking hands, Gerda gulped the magic liquid down. At first she felt nothing, and then suddenly she felt dizzy and everything began to spin. Gerda found herself traveling through space into the heart of the northern lights. Amazing bright colors swirled all around her like mysterious ghostly dancers. Then everything returned to white as they passed to the other side.

Gerda found herself standing on a vast open plain of ice with the reindeer and the raven. Before their eyes stood the Snow Queen's palace in all its terrible, brilliant beauty.

Gerda looked on in awe and fear. Jagged pillars of ice pointed up into the night sky.

"She knows you are here, Gerda," said the crow. "She will try to stop you."

"It's so cold," shivered Gerda, and she stood as if frozen to the spot.

A low rumble filled the air, and the ground began to shake. The cracking snow trembled and split, then rose into terrifying living snow creatures.

"The Snow Queen's guardians," cawed the raven. "They must be defeated!"

The terrible beasts pounded forward, baring their icy teeth. Gerda was gripped with fear, and the raven squawked in alarm. Suddenly the reindeer jumped and lowered his great antlers. One by one the snarling beasts were smashed to powdery snow.

At last Gerda stood at the entrance to the Snow Queen's palace. Its cold silence crept upon her like icy fingers. Towering ice walls stretched upwards and touched dark spaces above. Icicles hung at crazy angles, sharp like frozen daggers. There was no peace in this bare place, only stillness, cold, and death. And from the shadows the Snow Queen watched, smiling in cold victory.

At the centre of a frozen lake lay Kay's lifeless body. His skin was pale and bloodless-blue; death was nearly with him. The Snow Queen moved to look at the child, and smiled at his surrender. Then she bent for one last frozen kiss that would make him hers forever.

"NO!" screamed Gerda, as she ran into the palace towards the frozen lake and Kay.

The mighty Snow Queen raised her head, and turned to face the girl. The force of her terrible, unearthly power threw Gerda to her knees.

"I have no strength to fight her with," thought Gerda, but then she remembered the words of the king. "You have a power far greater than hers… It comes from your heart."

And Gerda felt how dearly she loved Kay, and her strength began to grow. The Snow Queen summoned all the winds of the world and threw them at the girl. But the power of Gerda's love was strong, and the tempest left her untouched.

The Snow Queen raged and shrieked with anger. Her screams echoed through the vast frozen palace. Her eyes glittered with icy fire, as she twisted into the furious winds, then spiraled upwards. And then she was gone. The swirling winds stopped, and there was a sudden calmness. Nothing remained of the Snow Queen.

Gerda ran to rescue Kay, but his body was like stone. His blank eyes stared into a place that Gerda could not reach. She thought that her friend was lost and that nothing could ever bring him back.

"Please, Kay, wake up. Don't leave me," Gerda whispered.

Desolate tears stung Gerda's eyes, and one teardrop splashed onto Kay's cheek. Slowly life returned to him where none had been before. The hardened, gripping cold relaxed, and the Snow Queen's spell was broken. Gerda's love had saved poor Kay and made him live again.

He blinked and looked around, as if waking from a sleep. "Gerda, where have you been?" he shivered. "What is this place. It's so cold?"

Gerda was filled with such happiness at Kay's return to life.

"Kay, oh Kay, you're alive!" she cried.

But Gerda knew she had to get him out of the palace quickly. "Hurry. We must leave now," she said, as she helped Kay to his feet. "The Snow Queen has gone but we are still in great danger—the palace is collapsing."

All around them the palace creaked, its ice columns groaned and cracked. The great halls shook, and ice walls splintered, smashing to the floor. Gerda and Kay ran outside, and huddled together with the reindeer and the raven. Safe from harm, they watched as bit by bit the Snow Queen's palace crumbled and crashed to the earth, until nothing was left but a cloud of snow that was whisked away by the wind.

And so the Snow Queen was defeated by Gerda's love for Kay. The darkness was gone, and the rising sun warmed their skin, reminding them of happier places.

"Let's go home, Kay," said Gerda.

Kay and Gerda left the frozen north behind. They climbed on to the back of the reindeer, and set off on the long journey home.

In the little town spring had arrived, and the trees were heavy with sweet-smelling blossom.

The flowers turned to greet the sun, and the world was warm again.

Kay and Gerda arrived home at last, tired but very happy.

"Let's go and find Mother," laughed Gerda. "I've missed her so much. I can't wait to see her again."

The two friends set off down the street, arm in arm.

Gerda's mother was coming out of her house, when she saw two familiar figures walking down the street.

"Oh my darlings, my little children! I didn't think I'd ever see you again," she cried with joy, hugging her two lost children.

For Gerda's mother had come to think of Kay as a son, and she loved him just as much as her own daughter.

Time passed on and memory with it, and soon the Snow Queen was forgotten. Gerda and Kay lived in endless summer, for they were happy and the best of friends again.

THE END

This edition published in 2006 by Carlton Books Ltd
20 Mortimer Street, London W1T 3JW

First published in the UK in 2006 by BBC Children's Books
BBC Children's Books is an imprint of Children's Character Books Ltd, 80 Strand, London WC2R 0RL
Children's Character Books Ltd is a joint venture company between Penguin Books and BBC Worldwide
Text and design © Children's Character Books 2006
The Snow Queen logo © SQ Productions/Amberwood Productions 2005

1 3 5 7 9 10 8 6 4 2

Retold by Melanie Joyce, based on the original story by Hans Christian Andersen and
adapted from the 2005 BBC film script of "The Snow Queen", written by James Andrew Hall
An Intro film, produced by Total Eclipse Television, PKJ Music and Amberwood Productions
Licensed by BBC Worldwide Ltd
Imagery created by Intro

Printed in Singapore